Madison's Patriotic Project

Teach Your Children Well

By Dr. Vanita Braver
Illustrated by Carl DiRocco

STAR BRIGHT BOOKS
NEW YORK

Published in the United States of America by Star Bright Books, Inc., New York.
The name Star Bright Books and the Star Bright Books logo are registered trademarks of Star Bright Books, Inc. Please visit www.starbrightbooks.com.

ISBN-13: 978-1-59572-110-5

Printed in China (MC) 9 8 7 6 5 4 3 2 1

Library of Congress Cataloging-in-Publication Data

Braver, Vanita.
  Madison's patriotic project / by Vanita Braver ; illustrated by Carl DiRocco.
      p. cm. -- (Teach your children well)
  Summary: Madison is disappointed when her patriotic scrapbook does not win first prize in the class contest, but eventually she realizes that she learned a lot from her project and feels proud that she worked hard on it.
  ISBN-13: 978-1-59572-110-5 (hardcover)
  ISBN-10: 1-59572-110-X (hardcover)
  [1. Contests--Fiction. 2. Schools--Fiction.] I. DiRocco, Carl, 1963- ill. II. Title.

PZ7.B73795Map 2007
[E]--dc22
                                        2006036047

To Alyssa, India, and Samantha, with love.
Thanks for being the best Tinker Bell, Baby Bear,
and Doodle in the whole wide world. —VB

To all my nephews and nieces,
a terrific bunch of kids. —CD

"Mommy, look, look!" Madison called as she
ran into the house. She handed her mother a note.
"It's from my teacher."

Madison's mom read, "For President's Day, our class is having a contest. Everyone should make a patriotic project and bring it to school on Friday. The student with the most creative project will win a prize and a gift certificate for Pete's Pizza Palace."

"I know what I am going to do," said Madison. "We learned that 'patriotic' means loving your country, so I'll make a scrapbook about America."

That evening, Madison told her dad all about the contest. "I just know I am going to win, Dad," she said.

"I know you'll do a great job, Sweetie, but remember, everyone in your class hopes to win," replied her dad. "There will be many good projects."

After dinner, Madison and her dad looked through some old magazines. Madison cut out a picture of the American flag, and one of the Statue of Liberty.

"Look, Madison," said her dad, "here's George Washington."

"Did he invent dollar bills?" asked Madison.

Madison's dad laughed. "No, Sweetie. Washington's portrait is on the dollar bill because he was our first president. And before that, he was a general in our fight for independence."

"A general! He must have been as brave as Courage," said Madison, and she gave her toy lion a quick hug.

By Thursday, Madison was ready to put her scrapbook together. She pasted the pictures onto construction paper. Next, she asked her dad to help write the captions. Under George Washington's portrait, Madison asked him to write, "George Washington was the first President of the United States."

Last, Madison tied all the pages together with red, white, and blue yarn.

"My scrapbook is perfect!" she crowed. "I just know I am going to win."

"Madison, you've done a great job," said her dad, as he looked through the scrapbook. "Even if you don't win, you learned a lot."

But Madison didn't hear him. She was thinking about the prize.

On Friday, Madison wiggled in her seat. She could hardly wait for her teacher to announce the winner. She could almost taste the pizza!

At last, Mrs. Petillo said, "Thank you all for your hard work. It was not easy to choose the best project. They are all so good! Everyone will get a certificate."

Madison's heart went "thump-thump." She almost called out, "But who won?"

Mrs. Petillo went on, "And the winner is. . ."
"Oh, boy," thought Madison. "This is it!"
She held her breath.

". . . Jonathan, for his beautiful collage!"
said Mrs. Petillo. "Let's all give Jonathan
a big round of applause!"

Tears welled up in Madison's eyes.
She could barely clap. She put her
head on her desk when Mrs. Petillo
gave Jonathan his prizes.

Somehow, Madison held in her tears.

"Oh Mommy!" sobbed Madison, as she burst through the door, "I didn't win! Jonathan got a blue ribbon and the pizza dinner. All I got is a stupid certificate."

Madison picked up Courage the Lion, and fell into her mom's arms.

"Honey, you can't win every time," Madison's mom cooed. "Even George Washington didn't win all his battles. The important thing is that you tried your best."

"Jonathan's collage was really ugly!" wailed Madison.

"That's not nice!" scolded her mother. "I'm sure Jonathan worked very hard on his project."

Madison sniffled.

"And I know you worked hard, too," her mom added. "How would you like to go to Pete's Pizza Palace tonight?"

"No," pouted Madison. "I didn't win, and anyway, Jonathan will be there." She turned away and stomped upstairs.

In her room, Madison thought about
how hard she had worked. She had been so
proud of her scrapbook when she finished it!
She looked at Courage the Lion and said,
"You know, I made a really good scrapbook."
Then she went downstairs to the kitchen.

"How are you doing, Sweetie?" asked dad.

"I'm okay," said Madison, "Mom said we
can go to Pete's Pizza Palace for dinner.
Can we still go, please?"

At dinner, Madison had two slices of pepperoni pizza. For dessert, she had her favorite, vanilla ice cream. Everything was yummy, and Madison felt much better.

As they were leaving, Madison saw Jonathan and his family.

"Hi, Jonathan," said Madison. She felt a little shy.

"Hi," said Jonathan, wiping pizza sauce off his face.

"Your collage was really good," said Madison. "See you Monday."

"Thanks!" he said, as Madison ran back to her parents.

At bedtime, Madison asked, "Mom, can we have pizza again tomorrow?"

"I don't think so," laughed her mother. "Pizza for dinner is a special treat."

"My scrapbook was pretty special, too, wasn't it?" asked Madison.

"Yes, it was, Honey," answered her mom. "And it was nice of you to tell Jonathan that you liked his collage."

Madison's mom tucked her in and kissed her. "Sweet dreams. I love you."

"Good night, Mommy," replied Madison. "I love you too."

Madison closed her eyes and then slowly opened them. She picked up Courage the Lion and cuddled him next to her.

Courage whispered into Madison's ear, "You should feel good about yourself, especially because you tried your best."

And with that, Madison closed her eyes and fell asleep.

Parents' Note

Dear Parent or Educator,

As a mom of three, an educator, and a practicing child and adolescent psychiatrist, I know that parenting is challenging at best; I have often said that I was the perfect parent until I had children!

I want what we all want for our children—to have them lead happy, enriching, and successful lives. But no matter who we are, the essence of being human is to undergo a wide range of experiences, both good and bad. Life presents us all with moral dilemmas, discrepancies of the heart and mind. How we live our lives and cope with difficult circumstances is a reflection of who we are and the choices we make.

One of life's greatest gifts is the ability to reflect, to ask questions of each other and of ourselves. Through this process, we learn to make good choices—and it's a gift that must be nurtured and learned. The *Teach Your Children Well* series models the dialogue and interactions that facilitate the critical thinking and self-reflection necessary for kids to learn to make moral, ethical choices.

We can make a difference in the world through the way we, as individuals, conduct our lives. Our children are really our greatest resource!

Warmly,
Dr. Vanita

Ten Tips for Raising Moral Children

1) Make raising moral children a priority. If you really want to raise moral children, then commit to it and put forth the effort.

2) Live by setting a moral example. Research has shown that parents are the most significant and powerful influence in their children's moral development.

3) Be clear about what you value, and communicate that. You can't adequately instill a belief in your children if it's not clear within you.

4) Set clear, reasonable, and challenging guidelines about what you expect from your children. Reinforce these at every opportunity, but be open to discussion.

5) Set clear boundaries and enforce limits. Understand that all children will test limits, and be consistent in your responses.

6) Recognize opportunities to teach. The most powerful and persuasive moral teaching opportunities present themselves in ordinary moments.

7) Emphasize the Golden Rule. Encourage your children to treat others the way they wish to be treated.

8) Reflection is a powerful, effective tool to stimulate internal motivation. Encourage your children to think through the consequences of their actions and their effects on others.

9) Reinforce positive behaviors. When your children make good choices, notice their behavior and express to them how it made you feel.

10) Listen actively and allow your children to think through dilemmas. Ask them questions that allow them to draw conclusions.